SAMUEL
SCAREDOSAURUS

Published in 2015 by Wayland

Text copyright © Brian Moses
Illustrations copyright © Mike Gordon

Wayland
338 Euston Road
London NW1 3BH

Wayland Australia
Level 17/207 Kent Street
Sydney, NSW 2000

Senior editor: Victoria Brooker
Creative design: Basement68
Digital colour: Molly Hahn

British Library Cataloguing
in Publication Data:

Moses, Brian, 1950-
 Samuel Scaredosaurus. --
  (Dinosaurs have feelings, too)
 1. Children's stories--Pictorial
  works.
 I. Title II. Series III. Gordon, Mike,
  1948 Mar. 16-
  823.9'2-dc23
ISBN: 978 0 7502 8086 0

Printed in China

Wayland is a division of
Hachette Children's Books,
an Hachette UK company.
www.hachette.co.uk

SAMUEL
SCAREDOSAURUS

Written by

Brian Moses

Illustrated by

Mike Gordon

WAYLAND

That strange shape beneath
the sheets is Samuel Scaredosaurus.

He doesn't like it when Mum turns his
light out at night. He imagines that his
dressing gown on the door is a pterodactyl
with folded wings.

Before Samuel falls asleep at night, he asks his Dad to look beneath his bed to make sure there's nothing there.

Samuel doesn't like hearing strange
noises when he's alone...

...although he knows there
is usually a sensible explanation.

Samuel is frightened of being lost. It happened to him once in the Bronto Burger Bar when he couldn't find his parents.

Happily, they found him.

He's scared too, when somebody says
that there's a big bully dinosaur about.

But he has learned
to hide himself
really well.

Samuel is scared when he first tries out
a new trick at the bone board park.

Or when he's on a ride at Dinosaur Island.
(His Dad pretends he isn't
scared, but Samuel
is sure he is!)

Samuel's Mum and Dad know all
about how scared he can be. They always
listen carefully and calmly when he
talks about his fears.

They tell him that sometimes
they feel scared, too.
His Mum says that
she is scared
of heights
and can't stand
on top of tall cliffs.

But that doesn't
frighten Samuel.

His Dad says how he was
often scared of going
to school.

But Samuel loves his school.

One day, Samuel's Dad said, "I know what we need to do. We need to turn you into a superhero. Let's call you, 'The Masked Dinosaur!'"

"I like that idea," said Samuel.
"But superheroes are brave, and I'm not."

"To begin with then, we'll make him your superhero friend. He can help you fight your fears."

"When you're frightened of what's under
your bed, think of the Masked Dinosaur.
He can defeat anything."

"Maybe we can make fun of what frightens you," his Mum said. "Imagine that the pterodactyl behind
your door is wearing
a funny hat."

"Or maybe he's doing a silly
dance across the room."

Perhaps you have a special word
that sounds powerful like 'ZAP' or 'POW'
and when you say it, your fear disappears.

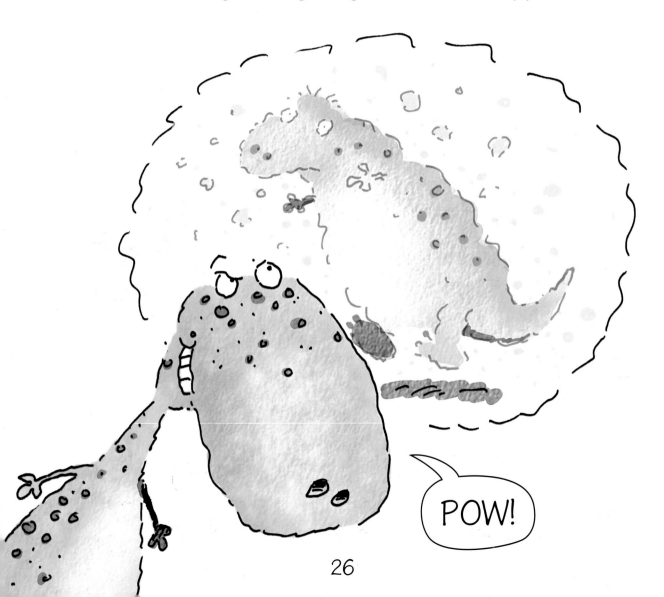

And if you're scared of the rides at Dinosaur Island, imagine the Masked Dinosaur sitting beside you, keeping you safe.

So Samuel tried to do what his parents said, and he used his special words. Then slowly but surely, Samuel became a little braver, then a lot braver...

...until Samuel Scaredosaurus really did turn into a SUPERHERO himself.

NOTES FOR PARENTS AND TEACHERS

Read the book with children either individually or in groups. Talk to them about what makes someone scared. How do children feel when they are scared? Do they feel like a wobbly jelly on a plate, or a shivering mouse that has just been seen by a cat?

Help children to write poems about the way they feel when they feel scared. Ask what scares them the most and use this as a first line for the poem.

> I am scared of the dark like...
> > a mouse is frightened of a fierce cat,
> > like a settee is terrified of a puppy's teeth,
> > like a fox is petrified of a hunter's gun,
> > like a car is afraid of the scrap heap.
> I am scared of the dark.

Then get them to compare their feelings with those of other creatures and even objects. Try to get children to use alternatives for 'scared' in each line.

Quite often children will reveal their worries when doing something with you, rather than in a face-to-face talk. Be ready to listen at any time. When a child talks about his or her worries it can help for parents and teachers to talk about what worried them when they were young. Tell children how these fears were overcome.

Sometimes it can help if children draw their fear. Maybe one picture might show the child in a scary situation while a second shows the child dealing with the situation. Thought bubbles could show what the child is thinking in each situation. Talk about how negative thoughts can change to more positive ones as the child loses that fear.

It helps Samuel to imagine a superhero who will sort out his fears for him. Ask children to think what their superhero would look like and to try to draw him or her. If your child is a Harry Potter fan there might me a word that could be said as a spell to banish fears.

Explore the notion of fear through the sharing of picture books mentioned on page 32. Talk to children about their fears and reassure them that it is natural to be scared occasionally and that everyone gets frightened from time to time.

BOOKS TO SHARE

Bella and Monty: A Hairy, Scary Night by Alex T. Smith
(Hodder Children's Books, 2009)
Bella and Monty are best friends but Bella is brave
and Monty is a great BIG scaredy cat!

Brave Mouse by Michaela Morgan (author)
and Michelle Cartlidge (illustrator) Frances Lincoln, 2010.
Lots of things frighten little mouse but he learns to stand
up for himself.

I Feel Frightened by Brian Moses (author)
and Mike Gordon (illustrator) Wayland 1993.
Looking at feeling frightened in an amusing, but reassuring, way.

The Elephant Who Was Scared by Rachel Elliot (author)
and John Bendall-Brunello (illustrator) QED Publishing, 2012.
When Little Elephant loses his mother
in the scary jungle he finds a leopard
cub who is also lost and together
they find their way home.